TEENAGER'S

TEENAGE YEARS ARE ALSO CALLED ADOLESCENCE

RAJAN YADAV

Dedication

This book is for all those who are in teenage, for the ones who are afraid of the teenage, this is also dedicated to everybody I know as teenager.

who was an inspiration in my writing's? I think God wants me to do something good and I thank him the most.

Hare krishna!!

Contents

Acknowledgements

Thank you to everyone who all were a part of my life and a big heartful Thanks to all those who are a part of me and my life.

Great! Great! thanks to my brother, I am glad to have a brother like Gopal. Gratitude to all my dear teen friends, sir and my family. *Also a special thanks to one of my friend who always insisted me to write, and was excited for my book too..!*

Foreword

This book brings you all the information about how teenagers face their adolescence and what is actually teenage years. Teenage is the period where people always lack behind in delivering correct information to their juniors, but in this book you will find many more things discussed like:

·Who are called teenagers/adolescence?

·What makes adulthood different from teenage?

·What do teenagers feel when they are in love?

·Control on feelings and emotions Teen friends during adolescence.

·Some important things for Teenagers to remember

·Why do teenagers get stressed so much?

·What is love?

·What is good relationship?/What makes it good?

·Break ups

·Moving on

Preface

In today's world teenagers are lacking behind because of a poor guidance or information's. sometimes as a senior also, we can't provide the needful information even we feel uncomfortable in sharing or experience to them.

But do you know, awareness rising is powerful because it educates people about topics which are new to them and recognise them to participate in regular activities. It's important for teenagers to understand and talk about how learning and thinking difference, affect daily life. This can help them become effective self advocates, speaking up for what they need in a positive way.

Teens with learning and thinking difference can be quick to criticize themselves and also self awareness means recognising positives as well as negatives. One should not fall in any type of misconceptions but always try to correct it.

This book brings you all the information about how teenagers face their adolescence and what is actually teenage years. Teenage is the period where people always lack behind in delivering correct information to their juniors, but in this book you will find many more things dscussed.

Teenager's

<u>Who are called teenagers/adolescence?</u>

Teenager the word itself says many things about the human beings at their adolescence, like teens or the teenagers are those who are of the age ending with "Teen"(I mean their age number ends with 'teen').
When human beings become 13 years of age they are then called as teens. And this teenage ends at the age of 20 years. In short we can only call someone as teenager when they are between 13 and 19 years old. But at some places teenagers who are 18 and 19 years old, they are also known as both teenagers as well as adults.

Sometime people also get confused between the words teenager and adolescence the words Mean the same but slightly different from each other. Like for example teenager means the the person who is having the age number ending with teen. Where as adolescence means the time period required for transition from childhood to adulthood.

It is also said that life of teenager changes daily. A teenager is everyday exposed to new ideas learning new things like emotions, experience from everyday's life, some good and some bad behaviours. Teenagers develop some kind of interest in several things. Before they enter the Teenage they are likely to focus on school, playing, studying and from all these they gain the parents approval of trusting them. The right time for gaining parents trust and approval is the time period before the teenage and once you gain their trust before the Teenage your teenage becomes smooth and a bit easier because your parents trust you.

What makes adulthood different from teenage?

But in some countries the adulthood is considered as the 18 years. This is because it is believe that an adult is a person who is eligible to take their own decisions without the help of their parents and someone elder. And also the responsibilities sometimes make a person adult before the time period. But the real adulthood is when a person crosses its teenage and completes its childhood. when a person complete its 19 years then he or she can be legally called as an adult.

And biologically a person is considered as an adult only when they are physically and sexually mature. This means that they have started or have passed the physical puberty and are able to sexually reproduce. By the way person is considered as a full grown adult only when they are in their middle of twenties. Some countries allow their citizens to have the authority to be an adult after a certain age limit and that is 18 years.

18 years is the age where you are legally allowed to do the things that an adult can do. Like for example; you can have your voter ID and vote, you get a right to drive vehicles and have a driving licence, and also can go for the jobs and so on. There are many more additional laws that tells from what age a person is allowed to do something.

Anyways now we know, who are teenagers and who are called an adult, also difference between them.

What do teenagers feel when they are in love?

Sometimes you can't write some things, can't speak but just feel it. Like being with someone, is like having the best filling in the world. Sometimes it so happens that you get a sense of your self with his words, such a self that gives you a sense of peace. But I think that sometimes a person ruins his own happiness, that's because everything will be going well between you, and one day a pile of misunderstandings will come from somewhere and everything will end. Still, you will hear his/her voice, whenever you remember him/

her and then you will feel that there is someone who is speaking very beautifully. But what is it that some things can look beautiful only in dreams.

Now look, those who fight with you meet many and will also meet in future, but those who fight for you will get very few and they will be very special to you (like your parents). I say this because it always happens that the one for whom you will fight will leave you alone one day, you must have heard such things from the mouth of many. But what a perfect line is said in hindi which everyone should remember is: "**वक्तपडातोजानछुड़ाली, जानसेप्यारेलोगोंने.**" This line is such that you find many people around you only during your happy days not in your bad days.

Now what happens is that when we fall in love, it is not our fault, it is just a natural filling that emerges with increasing age. Now if I want to say something about this, I probably won't be wrong. Yes I agree this teenager's life is very difficult, but this is just a age, which will slowly pass with time. And if the same thing is said in the language of science, then it will be such that there are some hormones which are released with increasing age and just because of this we have such thoughts and maybe you do not have much control over them and If it happens, then nothing is better for you then this.But as far as I know it is natural, it should happen with everyone, and if it is not happening then you must visit the doctor once.

Control on feelings and emotions

As soon as we enter the teenager years we start getting all those kinds of feelings from which we were unknown until now, so let's see what it is actually. Like we all know that the Teenage year starts probably from 13 and ends at 19 years. so to understand it more clearly let us divide the ages into two phase that is Phase 1 and phase 2.

PHASE-1 includes the age group from 13 to 15 years of teens. where you can see that this age group teens have just entered the Teenage years and this shows that they are immature teens, because the surrounding has just changed according to the comfort zone.

However at this phase the teens should try to control their emotions, feelings and etc. because this is the age where most of the teenagers make mistakes by not having control over there emotions and feelings because of which get distracted from their goals. I strongly advised not to fall in the trap of relationships at this phase(Phase 1), because Phase 1 has the high chances of distractions.

phase-1

And the ege 16 is common type of teenagers for both the phrases(Phase -1 and phase - 2). Here some teenagers may become mature but some maybe still immature to understand environment. In short we can say that the age 16 works as a divider between phase -1 and phase -2 teenagers.

PHASE-2 includes the age group from 17 to 19 years of teens. where we find that the teenagers become mature enough to understand the environment and react accordingly. At this phase the control over the feelings and emotions is just required to keep yourself safe from harming yourself. Just because some teenagers at this phase, go for a deep love relationships and after getting dumped they practice illegal activities like suicides and also harm themselves. which is totally bullshit. This happens because attractions, feelings and also emotions are true at this phase-2.

phase-2

I agree that we can't have a control over the natural phenomenas occurring in our body but at the same time you should be able to control yourself from any kind of illegal activities.**"Having control on feelings is not that important but having control on your activity is most important".**

So here you get a bullet point that -**"Follow the time, to reach on time."**

Whatever is happening with you and around you just let happen because in this situation sometimes good happens or sometimes bad too. **"Every dark phase has another bright phase too."** So wait for your golden opportunity, which is soon to arrive.

And if seen, it also happens that sometimes we want something from life and we get something else in life. Like we love someone immensely and get immense hatred in return. But sometimes there are some relationships with which we are attached without any expectation, that means we do not want anything in return. We just fall in love with them, and some kind of relationship is formed with them which cannot be made with anyone else. I've also heard that **"If people don't accept you, don't be discouraged because people often give up things they can't pay for."**

It is in your hands to love someone but it is not in your hands to let the person in front of you to realize that love. But dearfriends, the greatest thing that happens is **"Whether the injury is on the heart or on the brain, there is pain."** And you have to bear those pains, because you create it and you are the reason for it. And also because you chose someone, if your choice is bad choice then it's your bad luck.

Teen friends during adolescence.

Talking about teenagers and if there is no talk about their friends, then it is impossible, so let's talk something about friends too. Having friends either boy or a girl makes no sense because every person has his/her own colours to show one day.

According to boys perspective, what do boys think is that

sometimes female friends are much better than the meal friends. In case of my experience 'I give it a approval'. I say this because female friends and male friends are not exactly 50-50 but maybe 60-40 in the term's of ratios. However everyone has his/her own experience so this all may vary from person to person. But at the same time getting a good female friend is more difficult than getting a good male friend.

Note:- *(Here female friend/male friend is not a girlfriend/ boyfriend, the word female friend or male friend is used to denote the friends in particular gender. And also the topic girlfriend/boyfriend will be discussed further).*

When we are in adolescence, then we have no one more than our friend, even some people love friends more than family members and believe a lot. In such a situation, having a good and true friend is very important. There is no doubt that we have many friends, but it is very important to know whether all are good and true or not. We can't make everyone our friends, can we? No we can't. First you know them and then make someone a friend.Because it is easy to fall into the wrong union, and it is equally difficult to get out of that wrong union. Well, it is a matter of how friends should be.Now let's talk about how to get good friends or how to be a good friend, at the same time we'll also try to know, who is how? A friend is not the one who pretends to be a friend, a friend is the one who does not make you feel alone. Even if you don't talk to him for months, this does not mean that you will not talk to friends for months now. It also doesn't matter if you don't meet a friend every day, but whenever you meet, it makes life beautiful.

There maybe some friends with whom even after talking every day, you feel like talking more and more. Well leave it, this is very common at this age. But what is the truth, you know? In this teenage we try to live a double character, because we show the world how happy we are, and we are living our life happily but when we look at ourselves or ourselves in the mirror, then we realise that how lonely, broken, and scattered we are. And we cannot even tell this thing to anyone except our friend. And if someone supports you at this time, then no one can be a better friend than him. And such friends should be respected, they should never be hurt.

Moreover, you will also find such friends who keep friendship with you only for their own means and some whom you keep for your own means. But there are some friends who are without means or selfishness. And these are your best friends who are there even in happiness and even when you are sad, they are there to support you. By the way, such friends who support you in your both sorrow and happiness are very few.There are some friends who are with you in happiness with pleasure, but leave you when the mountains of sorrow breaks. But there are some friends who are not in your happiness sometimes but when you are sad, they come first. And face the problem with you. Maybe they are called true friends.

Some important things for Teenagers to remember :-

When it comes to the sudden change in behaviour then it should be understood that the Teen is suffering from some kind of depressions or having lots of stress. And this depression and stress maybe because of certain things related either their past relationship, some kind of family issues, or it maybe regarding their academics.
So let us see what is depression. Whenever a teenager experiences break up in relationship, failure in exams, or in a particular activity then there arises depression. It also occurs when there is a death of loved one, that time they experience feeling of sadness, loss of someone special. Sometimes they feel so hopeless that they stop following their normal daily routine and feel like doing nothing. Sometimes you experience a short depression which is like, something had happened long back before, but you suddenly remember that things, that past and start feeling guilty about that particular incident. Here you feel yourself as a fault maker, you feel like why did that happen and why did I do that particular thing.
It may happen that you heat the person for doing wrong with you. But at sametime you feel some attractions to those things but not to the person. You feel attracted to those things because it included you in it.
At this moment the best action you should do is:-
1) Just forget those things.
2) Throw all those things which were related to that incident.(Because things which are gone is gone)

3) Move on.

Point number (3) is the best thing to be advised, from many people. It is because you not only move on in the new life but also make yourself comfortable. When you move on you find new happy things, new people and new memories which will obviously make you feel comfortable.

Sometimes, teen depression may result from environmental stress. Environmental stress means the situations, conditions which are in the surrounding. But whatever is the cause, when they are with their friends or family or doing things that the teen usually enjoys, but don't try to improve them, give them some space and take care but don't force to do anything. Which will make them angry and shout.

There are many reasons why a teenager might become depressed. For example: teens can develop the feelings of school performance, public status or the family life.

Why do teenagers get stressed so much?

Stress is what every human being have in their day to days life. Stress is the word which means "to be drawn tight " and also according to Richard lazarus "stress is a feeling experienced when an individual feels that the demands exceed the personal and social resources and individual is able to mobilize". I know this statement is not easy to understand in one take. So let us talk about it in simple way.

Stress is the common feeling which I think everyone has and no one can be skipped from it. Like you have stress,

when you need more time to reach the destination but you have very less time.
However this stress has nothing special to do with teenager's because, every human being have the stress in some or the other form. Either it is a small kid or an old man.
- when your exams are soon to arrive but you are not well prepared for it.
- when you wait for something to happen in your favour but it is not in your hands, and so no .

What is love?

love is when one person feel good about the other one and cares like no one doe's. Love is one knows the secrets about you and keeps it secret. when you feel comfortable in sharing all your secrets to them without any fear.You share all your deepest, darkest, most important talks. Love is also when you make mistakes and the person forgives you. Yeah it is said that "The mistakes can be forgiven but not forgotten".
First of all, loving someone or being loved by someone is the best feelings in the world during your adolescence. I said this because at this time you are the person who will always need one kind of important attention from someone, also a person who will always try to understand you and your problems and cares for you. And you get all these from love. Love helps you feel important understood and secured.
sometimes many of us feel that love is what we feel for a parents our brother/sister and their teachers, no this is not

love whatever we feel for them is the respect that we do in the form of love, the feelings which we have for our parents is totally different from the feelings we have for someone in our opposite gender whom we love.

Our ability to feel romantic towards someone is love, can be said shortly. And this feeling starts developing during adolescence. This can be noticed all over the world in the teenagers. Because this is the age period when teens feel attraction and it is a natural part of every teenager's life. So let us see how does it work in real life. Actually this word love is not enough to explain everything about love that is why we have some more words like: attraction closedness and commitment

Attraction it is all about your interest and someone you feel good about someone, you feel comfortable with someone. Like in many colleges professor says this as a fun that if your subject Chemistry is weak you can't have a good relationship. It is just for fun what professor create but, here the word chemistry is linked with love. Do you know why and how? Okay I'll tell it, having a good chemistry between two person can even create a love

Closeness: we all know that, when we feel attracted towards someone at that time this closeness plays the biggest role. It is all about the bond between two person, For example closense is the bond which develops on sharing thoughts and feelings that we don't share with anyone else. And when you have this kind of bond between your love one's then you feel comfortable, supported cared for, understood for everything. When bonding becomes strong than you are ready to be accepted for who you are. Also the main thing, trust is the biggest part of the bond developing. So try trusting on people but not on wrong people.

Commitment now when these two attraction and closeness get together or say, combines together then you make a commitment which is called as true perfect love.

Sometimes the teenager think that expressing your feelings is wrong, but it is not that. This is like it's your feeling what you feel and nothing is wrong in expressing your feelings. Yes it may hurt the person whom ever you express your feelings but it will hurt to those who don't have feelings like you have as an teenager. Everyone have got the right to feel not from human but by the nature itself.

For example if you like someone he or she has to like you in the same way is not possible. If you like someone you can express your feelings to him or her, but you can't force that person to like you back.

Sometime what happens you know? We like someone and we find that the person does not like us back in the same

manner (which is called as one sided affair or love). Now here we also see that if the person does not like you back as you do, then you indulge into any other unacceptable behaviour which is really bad and wrong.
But expressing your feeling is not wrong and if it is wrong, then why is it promoted too much in the society and public, why is it shown on the TV shows, television programs and many school college going students Love Stories. This is only promoted, so that the teenagers can learn to control themselves and keep themselves safe. So expressing your feelings is not wrong but following any unacceptable behaviour or a path is absolutely wrong part of teenagers life.

What is good relationship?

What makes it good?

Whenever a person fall in love it is always seen that they experience their first attraction and this attraction can be of any type.Teenager's at this stage they often daydream about a crush or new BF/GF. Good relationship can be built by only being a supportive, caring and knowing their likes and dislikes, dreams and worries, fears and weaknesses. If someone cares, that means they support you when you are in worries or afraid. Also they don't judge you and insult but they try to help you coming out of the problems.This is all what makes relationship God and better. But now let's see what ruins the relationship or ends the relationship.

Break ups

Mainly the relationships end due to misunderstandings. Same like friendships relationships also fail sometime if they are not given enough time and attention. Teenager's are always so busy with schools, extracurricular activities, that they always choose the way of going away from relationships and end up. sometimes they end it because of the different career path or going to separate colleges, separate streams. And for some teenagers the things change as they get adult and responsibilities on their head.

And also sometimes both the person end It by understandings and proper conversations. Some of them breakup when they find their partners cheating on them. Also some of them just leave the relationships, to get in a new relationship with other one and this happens when they find someone of their opinion or thoughts. Sometimes the one feels this way when the other one feel that Way Or other does not.Most of the time the teenagers just take advise from their friend and the friend advises in such a way that they end up with the relationships.

Moving on

MOVING ON

Now when teenager experiences the break up they need to move on, rather than staying stuck at one place with their past. And staying stuck at one moment shows the pain of losing someone special. Like the feelings of hurted early in the relationship shows the newness, rawness of the loss and it can be really very destructive. That is why they are called as Broken Heart When relationship ends people really need support because no one can be prepared for the upcoming loss. At this time they need close friends and family members to come out of it.

Unfortunately lots of people mainly adults, they expect that the teenagers should bounce back and just get over it. when the teenagers heart is broken they need people or someone who can really understand the pain, he is going through. love and relationship teachers us self respect as well as respect for others. love is one of the most full filling thing we can have in our lives.

Dear Dad

Whatever good I do is because of you,
There's lot to say but here is few.
You have loved me and held my hand since my birth,
Because there's no body, better than you on this earth.
You sacrifed a lot, that's the truth,
I'll follow you the same, when I'll grow up youth.
With no good health, you work day and night,
No matter what work you do,
because you make our lives beautiful and bright.
If I could write about you, It would be the greatest ever told,
I would write, my father is heart of gold.
I remember every lesson you teach and gift you Give,
I know the world is big, but my heart is where you Live.

-Rajan yadav

9 798887 046839

Printed by Libri Plureos GmbH in Hamburg,
Germany